THE INCREDIBLE HULK

HULK vs. HULK

by Mark Shulman
Illustrated by Louie De Martinis

Meredith® Books
Des Moines, Iowa

ISBN 0-696-22985-4

Bruce Banner walked slowly down a dark street. He was tired and worried.

It's been too long since I've turned into the Hulk, Bruce thought. *It's going to happen soon. I know it. What a curse to be the Hulk!*

That night, a familiar giant shadow appeared on the wall of the bank on Twenty-Fourth Street.

A powerful green fist swung through the air, punching a hole right through the bank's solid brick wall.

Minutes later, two big sacks of money shattered the bank window and tumbled onto the street. Then the massive figure disappeared into the shadows of the night.

Bruce Banner woke up to terrible news on the TV. "…Bank video cameras show the Hulk is the bank robber," said the reporter. "Police will now try harder than ever to catch the Hulk."
Bruce turned off the TV.

The Hulk has never committed a crime like this before, Bruce thought, as he searched his room for the stolen money. *Is it true?* He didn't want to believe Hulk would do such a thing. *I saw the video. It has to be true!*

The Hulk must have hidden the money, Bruce thought. *What do I do? Wait! I know. I'll use my own money to give back what the Hulk took. Then maybe the police will leave the Hulk alone.*

That afternoon, Bruce Banner walked into the bank. *They don't know I'm the Hulk*, he thought, but that did not stop him from feeling nervous.

Bruce was in line when there came a explosive crash that shook the entire building. It felt like an earthquake! *What was that?* Bruce wondered. He turned his head quickly. He didn't want anything exciting to turn him into the Hulk.

This time, the Hulk wasn't coming out of Bruce
Banner. The Hulk was coming through the bank wall!
  "It's the Hulk!" screamed the bank customers. They ran
for cover as huge, green arms broke through the wall.
"Run!"

Bruce could not run away. *How can this be the Hulk?* he thought, as he stared at the green monster. *It's not possible!*

When the dust cleared, Bruce knew how it *was* possible. This was an imposter —*a robot Hulk!*

I have to stop this monster! Bruce thought. *If I can just ….* But just then he was hit by a flying piece of brick.

Bruce was the only one who could stop the robot Hulk, and he was knocked out cold.

The robot Hulk walked to the bank's vault.

"Our weapons are useless!" cried the bank's guards.

The robot tore off the heavy-duty vault door with an ear-splitting *Rip!* of metal and threw it at the dazed guards.

The guards ran for their lives. And the robot Hulk grabbed bank bags with millions of dollars in cash and gold.

But suddenly, a new shadow appeared …

"You not Hulk!" roared the real Hulk, leaping at his robot enemy. "Me Hulk!"

The blow to Bruce Banner's head had turned him into the Hulk! But, would the real Hulk help the situation or make it worse?

Suddenly, the robot turned to defend himself. He grabbed a solid steel door and hurled it through the air. Hulk grew angrier.

"Hulk no need bad guy like you pretending! Puny humans hate Hulk too much already!"

Reaching up, the robot pulled down an entire shelf of solid gold bricks. With lightning speed, he threw one heavy brick after another toward the Hulk.

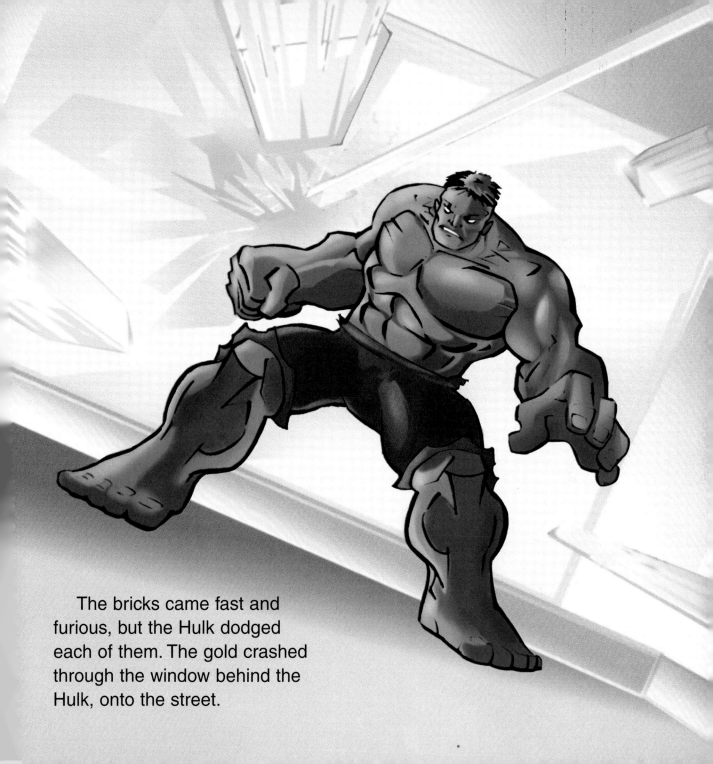

The bricks came fast and
furious, but the Hulk dodged
each of them. The gold crashed
through the window behind the
Hulk, onto the street.

Hulk moved closer to his enemy. "You look real good for a pretend Hulk," said Hulk, pinning the robot to the floor. "Now Hulk make you look bad!"

The robot struggled, but was outmatched. Hulk lifted him and smashed his robot legs into the ground. Gears and metal parts flew everywhere.

Hulk smashed the broken robot onto the bank floor. The robot didn't fight back. Instead, it threw more gold and a bag of money past the Hulk and out the window.

Hulk didn't let up. He delivered another crushing blow and then another! Hulk tore off the robot's arms and ripped out a handful of wires until the thieving robot's eyes went dark. "Now Hulk find your boss!"

Hulk jumped through the shattered bank window. He leapt toward a frightened little man holding a special remote control. The man was hiding in a pickup truck filled with gold and money.

"Hulk have enough trouble without YOU!" he yelled.

The police arrived seconds later.
They expected to find Hulk. Instead,
they found a long piece of green metal
wrapped around the real bank robber.
It was a going-away present from the
Incredible Hulk.